The SLUG PRINCE

To anyone who's ever kissed a slug

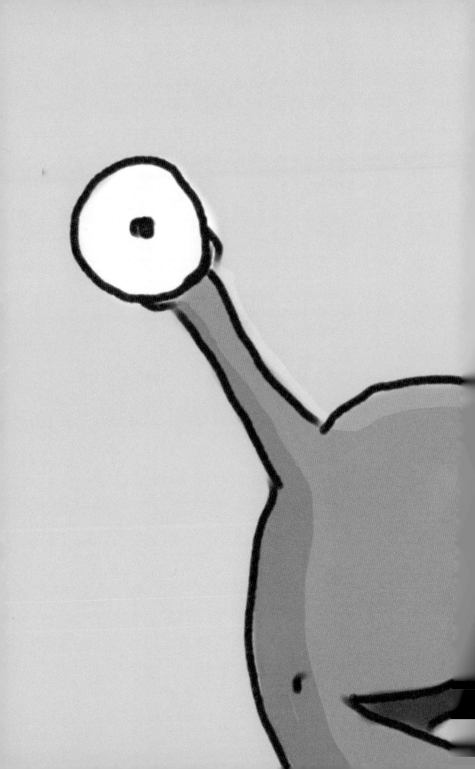

My name is Jean-Phillipe.

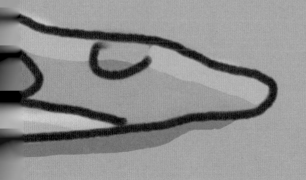

I am a PRINCE!

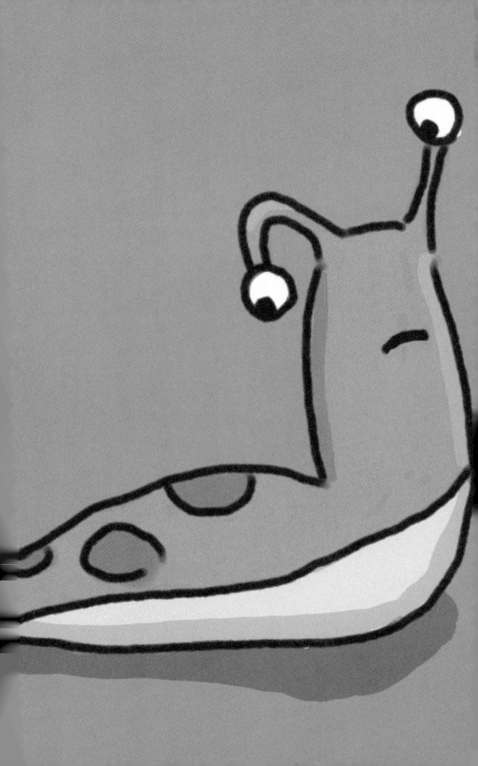

I see. You are fooled by my...er...unsightly exterior.

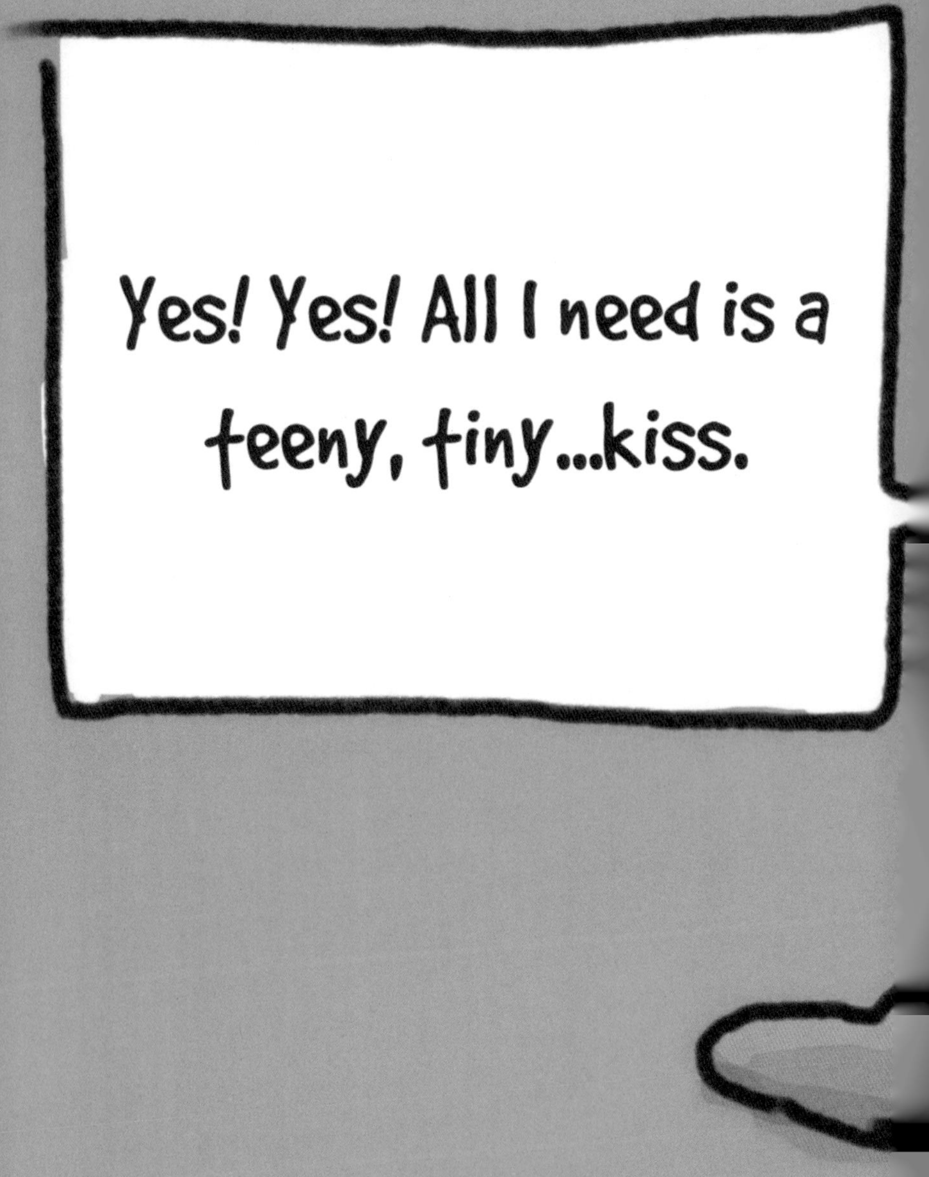
Yes! Yes! All I need is a teeny, tiny...kiss.

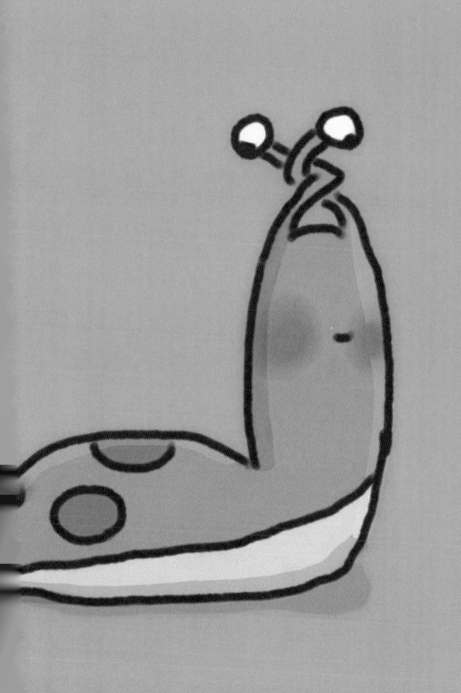

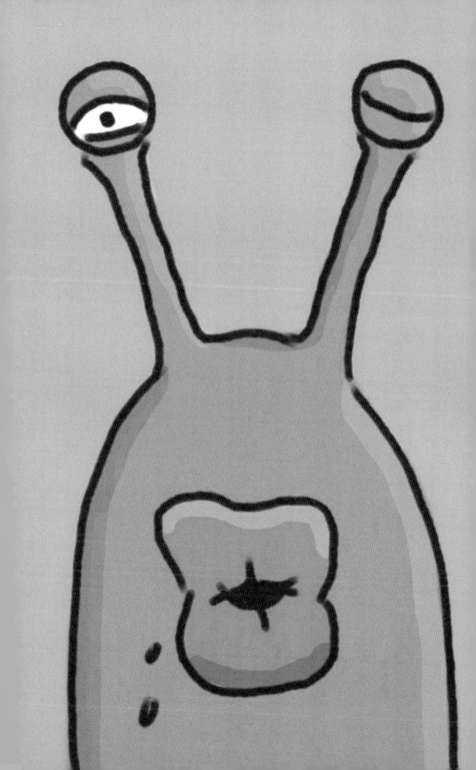

You are not kissing.

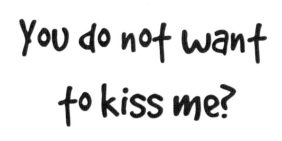

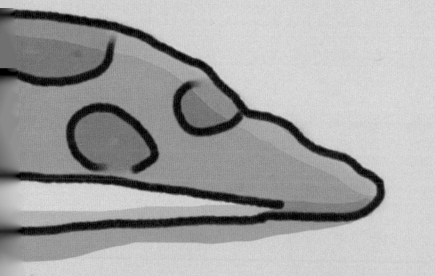

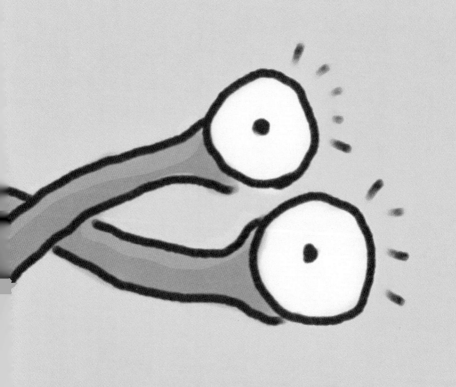

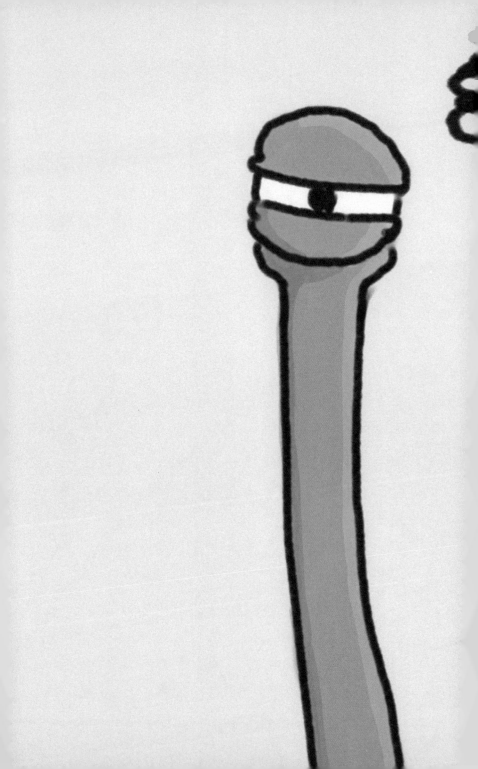

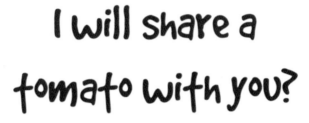

A strawberry?

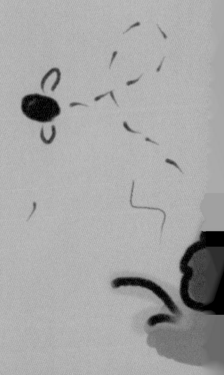

This lovely pile of poop?

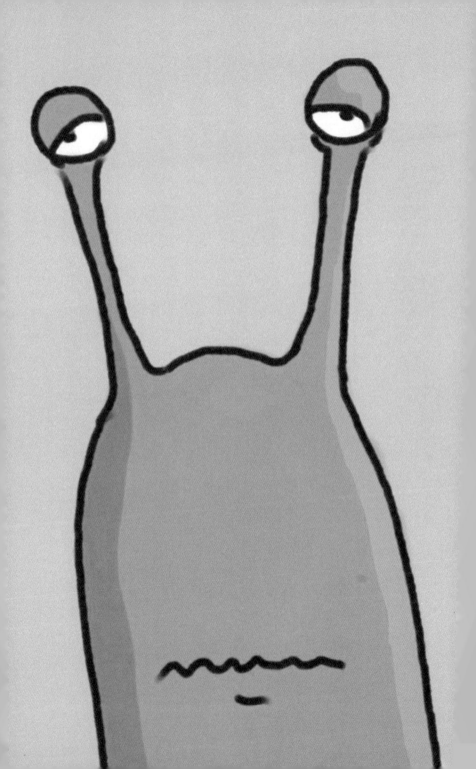

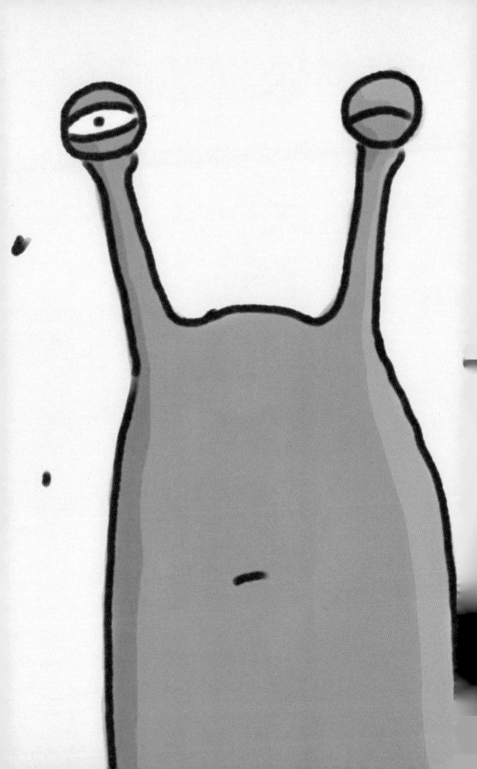

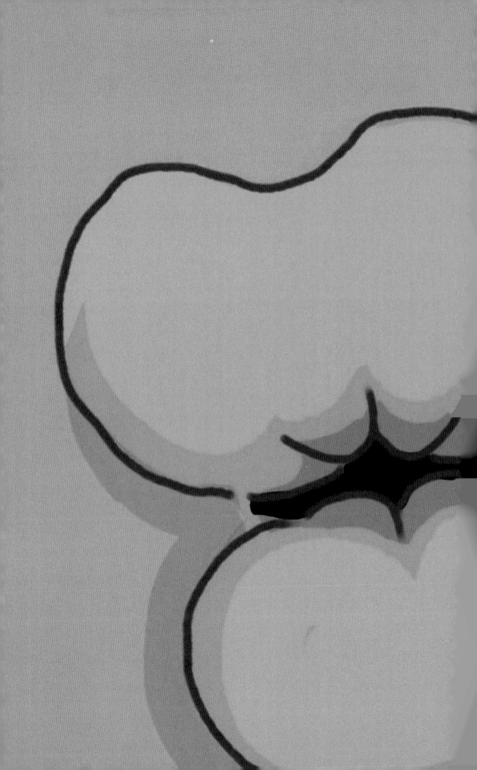

Ah ha! Now, you shall see that I have spoken the truth. First, please count to three.

Ta da! Aren't I the most dashing prince you have ever beheld? And to think, you did not belive me.

Now, how about another kiss?

Also by Martin Dale

Keep up with Martin's writing at:

www.martindalebooks.com